P9-CFA-309

Disney · PIXAR

# TOY STORY

## The Pet Problem

By
Kristen L. Depken

Illustrated by
Caroline LaVelle Egan

A GOLDEN BOOK • NEW YORK

Copyright © 2011 Disney/Pixar. All rights reserved. Slinky® Dog is a registered trademark of Poof-Slinky, Inc. © Poof-Slinky, Inc. Mr. and Mrs. Potato Head® are registered trademarks of Hasbro, Inc. Used with permission. © Hasbro, Inc. All rights reserved. Published in the United States by Golden Books, an imprint of Random House Children's Books, a division of Random House, Inc., 1745 Broadway, New York, NY 10019, and in Canada by Random House of Canada Limited, Toronto, in conjunction with Disney Enterprises, Inc. Golden Books, A Golden Book, A Little Golden Book, the G colophon, and the distinctive gold spine are registered trademarks of Random House, Inc.
ISBN: 978-0-7364-2698-5
www.randomhouse.com/kids
Printed in the United States of America
10 9 8 7 6 5 4 3 2 1

Buzz Lightyear and Sheriff Woody were very lucky toys. They lived with Bonnie, a little girl who loved to play. Every day, Bonnie and her toys had many amazing adventures together.

But one afternoon, Bonnie did not come home from school at her usual time.

"Where is she?" Rex asked.

"Don't worry—she probably had a playdate," said Woody.

Soon, the door burst open. Bonnie ran to her table and placed something on top of it.

"What is that strange metal contraption?" Buzz whispered to Woody.

They watched as Bonnie undid a small latch—

—and spun around with a small, furry creature in her hands.

Bonnie had brought home the Sunnyside Daycare classroom pet—a hamster named Harvey!

Bonnie cuddled the little animal, then ran out of the room with it.

"She'll never play with us now!" wailed Rex. "We're not cute and cuddly."

"Speak for yourself," replied Trixie.

"Calm down, everyone!" Buzz reassured them. "Bonnie's got a new pet, but we're still her toys."

That night, Bonnie didn't play
with her toys. She only played with
Harvey, the hamster.
She dressed him up . . .

and took him to a tea party.

She even kissed him goodnight.

When Bonnie left for school the next day, the toys decided they had to do something if they wanted her to play with them that night.

"I'll have a talk with the fuzzy little guy," said Woody. He began to fiddle with the latch on Harvey's cage.

"Umm, Woody, maybe you should keep that shut," warned Buzz.

But Woody opened the door—and the hamster zipped out of the cage, onto the floor, and out of Bonnie's room!

"Woody! How could you let him out?" cried Jessie.

"I didn't do it on purpose!" said Woody.

"Bonnie loves that hamster," said Buzz. "We've got to find him before she gets home from school."

Together, the toys tiptoed down the hall. Suddenly, a furry head poked out of a nearby doorway.

"I see him!" shouted Buzz.

Harvey darted away.

"Way to go, Captain Quiet," said Mr. Potato Head.

"Maybe we should split up," suggested Woody.

Hamm and Mr. Pricklepants looked in the laundry room. A sock was moving in the laundry basket! They climbed up to get a better look.

Suddenly, Hamm let out a huge sneeze.

He and Mr. Pricklepants toppled to the floor just as Harvey ran out of the room.

"Guess I'm allergic to rodents," Hamm said.

Trixie and Mr. Potato Head were looking under the beds when Trixie spotted two eyes peering at her.

She wiggled farther under the bed. And then . . . "Uh-oh—I'm stuck!"

Mr. Potato Head started tugging on Trixie's legs, until POP! He lost his arms!

The pair didn't even notice when Harvey darted away.

A few minutes later, Buzz and Jessie spotted Harvey with his head buried in the couch cushions. As they tiptoed toward him, Jessie accidentally activated Buzz's noisy laser.

The startled hamster jumped off the couch and ran away again.

All the toys met in the kitchen. They asked Chuckles if he had seen the hamster.

"Is he small, furry, kind of round?" asked Chuckles.

"That's him!" said Mrs. Potato Head.

"Nope—haven't seen him," said Chuckles.

Just then, the toys heard a noise coming from a cupboard. Woody opened the wooden door and found Harvey happily munching on some breakfast cereal.

"Okay, Harvey!" said Woody. "Time to go back to Bonnie's room."

But the hamster just kept nibbling on his cereal.

"Come on, little critter!" Jessie swung her lasso around the hamster and tugged gently. But Harvey wouldn't budge.

Suddenly, Buzz had an idea. "Everyone grab a few pieces of cereal, then follow me," he said.

Buzz began placing pieces of cereal in a line across the kitchen floor. He was making a trail! The other toys followed.

When the hamster saw the cereal on the kitchen floor, he climbed out of the cupboard and nibbled his way through the kitchen . . .

down the hallway . . .

around the corner . . .

into
Bonnie's
room . . .

and back into his cage.

The toys cheered. They were glad to have Harvey back where he belonged—even if that meant Bonnie wouldn't have time to play with them.

Suddenly, the toys heard a car door slam.

"Bonnie's home!" they cried. Everyone took their places as Bonnie burst into her room and ran to the hamster cage.

"Hello, Harvey! Are you ready to meet your new friends?" she asked.

The toys were surprised when Bonnie introduced them to the hamster one by one.

"We're all going to play together every day!" she said.

Soon, the toys loved Harvey just as much as Bonnie did.

"I think playtime is more fun with Harvey here," said Woody.

"You're right," Buzz replied. "But let's keep extra cereal around just in case."